HEY DIDDLE DIDDLE

Grolier Educational Corporation

Hey, diddle, diddle,

The Cat

and the Fiddle,

The Cow jumped over the Moon,

The little Dog laughed

to see such fun,

And the Dish ran away with the Spoon.

BABY BUNTING

Bye, Bye, Baby Bunting!

Father's

gone

a-hunting,

Gone to fetch

a Rabbit-skin

To wrap the Baby Bunting in.

ISBN 0-7172-9023-9

Printed in Portugal